CARTOON NETWORK®

# SCOOBY-DOO!™ AND THE PHONY FORTUNE-TELLER

Look for the Scooby-Doo Mysteries.
Collect them all!

- #1 Scooby-Doo and the Haunted Castle
- #2 Scooby-Doo and the Mummy's Curse
- #3 Scooby-Doo and the Snow Monster
- #4 Scooby-Doo and the Sunken Ship
- #5 Scooby-Doo and the Howling Wolfman
- #6 Scooby-Doo and the Vampire's Revenge
- #7 Scooby-Doo and the Carnival Creeper
- #8 Scooby-Doo and the Groovy Ghost
- #9 Scooby-Doo and the Zombie's Treasure
- #10 Scooby-Doo and the Spooky Strikeout
- #11 Scooby-Doo and the Fairground Phantom
- #12 Scooby-Doo and the Frankenstein Monster
- #13 Scooby-Doo and the Runaway Robot
- #14 Scooby-Doo and the Masked Magician
- #15 Scooby-Doo and the Phony Fortune-teller
- #16 Scooby-Doo and the Toy Store Terror

Written by
James Gelsey

Written by
James Gelsey

A
LITTLE APPLE
PAPERBACK

SCHOLASTIC INC.
New York Toronto London Auckland Sydney
Mexico City New Delhi Hong Kong

ISBN 0-439-18879-2



12 11 10 9 8 7 6 5 4 1 2 3 4 5 6/0

Printed in the U.S.A.
First Scholastic printing, March 2001

# Chapter 1

"Well, gang, we're almost there," Fred said as he drove the Mystery Machine.

"Man, the suspense is killing Scooby and me," Shaggy complained. "Why don't you tell us what the big surprise is already?"

"Okay," Fred said. "We're going on Cap'n Hornsby's Showboat. There's going to be a buffet, a show, and other groovy stuff."

"A boat? But what if Scoob and I get, like, seasick?" Shaggy complained.

"You won't get seasick," Daphne reassured him. "You'll be so busy having fun, you won't have time."

"Man, I hope you're right," Shaggy said.

Fred steered the Mystery Machine into a large parking lot. He found a parking space at the far end of the lot. The gang got out of the van and started the long walk to the pier. A big paddleboat was docked in the harbor.

"That must be Cap'n Hornsby's Showboat," Velma remarked. "It looks just like something out of a Mark Twain book."

"It was really nice of the guy at the van repair shop to give you these tickets, Fred," Daphne said.

"I know," Fred agreed. "He said he wanted to thank us for leaving him food every time the van needs work."

"So that's why our secret snack supply

keeps disappearing, Scoob," Shaggy whispered. "We'll have to find a new hiding place — one that's *not* in the van."

As the gang got closer to the pier, they found a short line of people waiting in front of a gate. A guard was checking tickets.

"This seems like a lot of security for a boat ride," Velma commented.

"That's because C. C. McGraw's on board," a woman standing in line said. She wore a smart blue suit with a green button on her lapel. "You know, the business tycoon whose companies are taking control of our lives."

"You must belong to P.I.L.," said Velma, noticing the green pin.

"I'm a founding member, actually," the woman said. "I'm Dorothy Cobb."

"What's P.I.L.?" Daphne asked.

"People for Independent Living," Dorothy explained. "Basically, we're dedicated to keeping big business from taking away our individual rights. Companies like C. C. McGraw's want to know everything that normal people do, so they can sell us better products. But they end up invading our privacy. P.I.L. wants to let people know what these companies are doing, so we can stop them."

The line started moving slowly.

"How do you do that?" asked Fred.

"Protests, rallies, letters to Congress, things like that," Dorothy said. "But we're not beyond taking more drastic action if necessary. For example, there are rumors that McGraw's invented a new kind of chip."

"Potato or chocolate?" asked Shaggy.

"Computer," the woman said. "From what I've heard, it'll revolutionize the whole business world, making it easier for people like C. C. McGraw to know everything that people like us are doing around the clock."

"So are you here to stop him?" Velma asked.

"No, just to take a pleasant boat ride," Dorothy said with a smile. "Unless, of course, the opportunity should present itself. Then there's no telling what I'll do." She showed the guard her ticket and walked through the gate.

"Like, I think it's time to abandon ship," Shaggy said weakly.

"Don't tell me you're getting seasick already," Velma said. "We haven't even gotten onto the boat yet."

"Or to the buffet," Daphne added.

"Besides, you wouldn't want Scooby to have to eat all that food by himself, would you?" asked Fred with a smile.

"I guess not," Shaggy said.

"Ranks, Raggy." Scooby barked and gave Shaggy a big, wet lick on his face.

"Man, you're worse than a tidal wave," Shaggy complained.

"No more fooling around, you two," Fred said. "Let's get on board."

# Chapter 2

The line moved slowly but steadily up the ramp onto the boat. As Scooby and his pals walked onto the boat, they were greeted by a short man wearing a captain's jacket. He had white hair and a bushy white mustache. He was wearing a white captain's hat, and he extended his right hand to shake everyone's hands.

"Good evening. I'm Cap'n Hornsby," he said warmly. "Welcome aboard."

"Thank you, sir," Daphne replied, shaking his hand. "I'm Daphne. And this is Fred, Velma, Shaggy, and Scooby-Doo."

"Pleased to meet you," Cap'n Hornsby said. "I hope you will enjoy yourself this evening. If there's anything I can do, please don't hesitate to ask."

"Just one question, Cap'n," Shaggy said.

"What's that, son?" asked Cap'n Hornsby.

"Which way to the buffet?" asked Shaggy.

"Shaggy!" Daphne scolded.

"That's all right, Daphne," Cap'n Hornsby said. "I'll have my First Officer show you the way." He turned to a tall man standing behind him. "Mr. Wagner, would you please show these young people to the buffet?"

But the man didn't seem to hear Cap'n Hornsby. He kept looking around and raising his left hand to his ear. It looked like he was talking to his wrist.

"Mr. Wagner!" shouted Cap'n Hornsby.

Startled, Mr. Wagner looked down at the captain.

"Sorry, sir," he said. "What did you say?"

"I asked you to show these nice young people to the buffet," Cap'n Hornsby said.

"But, Cap'n Hornsby, who will keep an eye on the passengers?" asked Mr. Wagner. "Mr. McGraw insisted on tight security this evening."

"I'm well aware of what Mr. McGraw insisted," replied Cap'n Hornsby. "But I'm the captain of this ship and have been for twenty-four years. I don't need all of your newfangled security gadgets to locate suspicious passengers. What I do need is for you to follow my orders. Right now, please."

"Yes, sir," Mr. Wagner replied. He looked at the gang. "This way, please."

"Thank you, Cap'n Hornsby," Daphne said.

The gang followed Mr. Wagner through the crowd and down a short flight of stairs

at the far end of the ship's deck.

"Twenty-four years is long enough, if you ask me," Mr. Wagner mumbled.

"What do you mean?" Fred asked.

"I mean that it's about time there was a change in leadership on this boat," Mr. Wagner replied. "I didn't come here to take orders from an unstable old man."

"He seemed perfectly charming to me," Daphne said.

"Whatever," Mr. Wagner said. "Here's your buffet. It's through there." He pointed to a door and then continued on his way.

"My, he wasn't very nice," Daphne commented.

"I'll say," Velma agreed.

"And I'll say something else," Shaggy added.

"What's that?" asked Fred.

"Let's eat!" exclaimed Shaggy.

# Chapter 3

The gang walked through the door and into the dining room. A huge ice sculpture of a sailboat stood on a round table in the center of the room. The table was piled high with different kinds of delicious-looking food.

"Let's go, Scoob, before the food runs out!" Shaggy cried.

"Rokay!" Scooby barked. The two of them ran over to the buffet tables.

"Where should we begin, pal?" asked Shaggy.

"I recommend you try the halibut," a man

said. Shaggy and Scooby turned around and saw a large, round man standing behind them. He had a thick brown mustache. "Of course, the salmon and shrimp are also good. As are the oysters, crab legs, and lobster."

"Thanks," Shaggy said. "But is there anything that's not so . . . so fishy?"

"Ah, a landlubber, eh?" the man asked. "Follow me." He led Shaggy and Scooby over to another table. "Roast beef, roast turkey, roast vegetables, all delectable." He started piling food onto his plate.

"Charles Cabot McGraw!" shouted a woman from across the room. In the blink of an eye, she was standing next to the man, taking his plate away.

"I must apologize for my husband," she said. "He sometimes gets carried away when it comes to food. I'm Mimi McGraw. And this is my husband, C. C. McGraw."

"Like, pleased to meet you," Shaggy said. "I'm Shaggy. And this is Scooby-Doo." Shaggy turned to look at Scooby, but he wasn't there.

"Scooby? Scooby-Doo, where are you?" called Shaggy.

They all looked over to the table and saw Scooby piling his plate high with food.

"Ah, a dog after my own heart,"

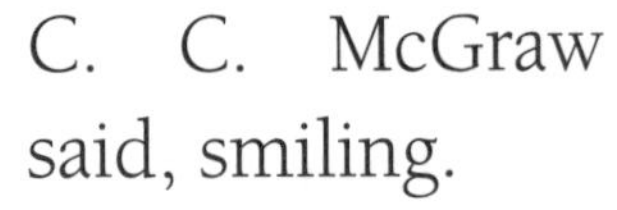

C. C. McGraw said, smiling.

"Speaking of hearts, you sure could use one," a man said to Mr. McGraw.

"What did you say?" asked C. C. McGraw sternly.

"You heard me," the man continued. "You could use a heart to pump blood through your veins instead of ice water. It would give you a little compassion for the rest of us trying to make a living in this world."

"I beg your pardon," C. C. McGraw huffed, "but do I know you?"

"I'm Floyd Mathewson," the man said. "I used to run a successful printing business. Until you and your megacorporation branched out into printing, that is. You put me out of business!"

"I can't help it if McGraw Industries brought about a change in your fortunes," Mr. McGraw replied.

"Well, get ready for a change in *your* fortunes!" Floyd Mathewson warned.

Fred, Daphne, and Velma walked over just in time to see Floyd Mathewson stomp out of the dining room.

"Jinkies, what was that all about?" Velma asked.

"Like, something about stealing ice from that guy's heart," Shaggy said. Velma gave him a puzzled look. "How can you expect me to pay attention with all this food around?" he said with a shrug.

"Please pardon my interruption," Dorothy Cobb said as she walked over. "But that is a beautiful locket, Mrs. McGraw."

"Thank you, my dear," she said. "My husband and I just celebrated our anniversary last night, and he gave it to me as a gift. And you are . . . ?"

"Dorothy Cobb," Dorothy said. "It's a pleasure to meet you."

"This is my husband, Charles McGraw," Mrs. McGraw said.

"I already know Ms. Cobb," Mr. McGraw said. "She pickets my office regularly."

"Excuse me," Mrs. McGraw interrupted. "But is your dog always that color?"

The gang looked over at Scooby-Doo. He sat with one paw holding his plate of food and his other paw covering his stomach.

"Scoob, are you all right?" asked Shaggy. "You're lookin' kind of green."

"I think he could use some fresh air," Mr. McGraw said. "Why don't we go up on deck until the show starts?"

"But what about the buffet?" asked Shaggy.

"Don't worry, son," Mr. McGraw said. "I'm sure there's plenty more where this came from."

# Chapter 4

The gang left the dining room and walked up the main stairs to the deck. The McGraws followed them. Shaggy led Scooby to one of the deck chairs. Fred, Daphne, and Velma stood by the handrail. The boat was moving slowly through the harbor.

"My, it's so pretty out here," Daphne said as she took a deep breath.

"Mmmm, nothing like the smell of the sea to put some spring back into your step," C. C. McGraw agreed. "Do you see that row of buildings over there?"

"You mean the ones with the colored lights on top?" asked Velma.

"Yup," said Mr. McGraw. "Those are all mine. The home of McGraw Industries. And starting tomorrow, things there will never be the same."

"What do you mean, sir?" asked Fred.

"I'll let you kids in on a little secret," whispered Mr. McGraw. "I've invented a new kind of computer chip so spectacular that it's going to change the face of business forever!"

"Charles!" scolded Mrs. McGraw. "You're not supposed to be talking about it. You said yourself that industrial spies could be anywhere."

"I know, but I have a good feeling about these young people," replied C. C. McGraw. "I can trust them. But I'm not so sure I can trust myself." He reached into his coat pocket and took out a small ring box. He opened it up and took out a tiny black square with little gold lines on it.

"You'd better hold this for safekeeping, dear," he told his wife. She took the object and put it into her purse. "And be careful. The whole future of the company is riding on that little piece of silicon."

"Now *that's* the first sensible thing you've done all night," his wife replied with a smile.

"C. C. McGraw did something sensible?" a man asked. "Impossible!"

Everyone turned and saw Mr. Wagner standing behind them.

"Wagner?" shouted Mr. McGraw. "What are you doing here? You have some nerve following me after I fired you. I ought to call the ship's security officer!"

"No need," replied Mr. Wagner. "I'm already here."

"You're in charge of security on this ship?" asked Mr. McGraw in disbelief. "But I fired you for stealing confidential information. I'm going to tell the captain."

"Go ahead, tell the captain," said Mr. Wagner. "With what I know, you'll all soon be working for me anyway." He smiled, then turned away and went belowdecks.

"I'm sorry you kids had to hear all that," Mr. McGraw apologized.

"How's your dog doing?" asked Mrs. McGraw.

"Retter," replied Scooby.

"Good," she said. "It always takes me a little time to get my sea legs, too."

"Like, I guess it takes dogs a little longer,"

joked Shaggy. "After all, they have four legs instead of two."

"Sometimes even us two-legged folks take a long time," Mr. McGraw added. "Look."

Everyone turned and saw Dorothy Cobb at the far side of the deck. She was holding onto the railing, and she did not look well at all.

"Well, I suppose we should be heading back downstairs," Mrs. McGraw said. "I believe the show will be starting soon. Why don't you kids sit with us?"

"Thank you, Mrs. McGraw," Daphne said. "What kind of show is it?"

"Ohhh, it's Madame Aurora," Mrs. McGraw said. "The famous fortune-teller."

"Man, I could have used her before I got on the boat. She could've warned me if I was going to get seasick," Shaggy said.

"I think the captain could have used her before you and Scooby got on board," Daphne said.

"What for?" asked Shaggy.

"To tell him if he had enough food for the two of you!" Daphne replied.

Everyone laughed as they walked belowdecks to the theater.

# Chapter 5

The gang and the McGraws quietly entered the theater and found the seats reserved for Mr. McGraw in the center of the audience. Onstage, a spotlight shone on the fortune-teller. She was wearing a long orange skirt and a flowered scarf around her neck. A woman in a dark green dress sat in a chair opposite her. A table with a crystal ball on it stood between them.

"That must be Madame Aurora," Daphne whispered.

"Before we look into the future, we must always look into the past," Madame Aurora said. She looked into the crystal ball. "I see you standing on the deck of the ship. You look ill."

"That's right, I was seasick when I came on board," the woman said.

"But there's more," the fortune-teller continued. "You will soon receive a sum of money."

"How?" the woman asked with great interest.

"It is hard to make out," Madame Aurora said. "I see numbers."

"That's amazing!" the woman exclaimed. "I won a raffle at the county picnic last week. I'm supposed to go pick up my prize tomorrow!"

The audience burst into applause. Madame Aurora bowed slightly.

"Now who would like their fortune told?" she asked.

"Watch this," Mr. McGraw whispered to the gang as he raised his hand.

"Yes, Mr. McGraw," called Madame Aurora. "What can I do for you?"

"I have misplaced something of great value to me," he explained. "And I can't find it anywhere. Can you help?"

Madame Aurora looked deeply into her crystal ball.

C. C. McGraw whispered to the gang, "I'm talking about the computer chip I gave to Mrs. McGraw for safekeeping. Let's see how good a fortune-teller she is."

"Yes, I see what you have lost," the fortune-teller said. "And to retrieve it, you must ask the man with the red rose."

"Who's the man with the red rose?" asked Mr. McGraw, puzzled at Madame Aurora's response.

Cap'n Hornsby stepped out onto the stage.

"That would be me, I think," replied Cap'n Hornsby. "My tie has a red rose design on it. And I have what you are looking for." He reached into his coat pocket and took out a wallet. "Someone found your wallet on the deck and gave it to me just before the show."

Mr. McGraw checked his own pockets.

"Well, I'll be," he said. "She's right. I lost my wallet. Thank you, Madame Aurora."

"Wow! I guess she *is* a real fortune-teller," Daphne said.

"But that is not all," Madame Aurora continued. "I see something bad happening in your future, something that will bring you great disappointment and pain." She stood up and walked over to the McGraws' chairs.

"What is it?" asked Mr. McGraw, growing concerned.

"The locket Mrs. McGraw is wearing," Madame Aurora said.

Mrs. McGraw put her hand to her necklace. "My goodness!" she exclaimed.

"If you continue to wear it, bad things will happen to you and your family," Madame Aurora replied. "The locket must be cleansed.

Put it into this bag, and I can help." She held up a small pouch made of silver cloth. It sparkled in the lights.

"Go on, Mimi," urged Mr. McGraw.

"But, Charles," protested Mrs. McGraw.

"No 'buts,' Mimi," said Mr. McGraw. "She knew about my wallet. Let's not take any chances."

Mrs. McGraw looked worried, but she unclasped her necklace and dropped the locket into the bag. Madame Aurora walked back onto the stage. She placed the bag down behind the crystal ball. The ball started glowing and white smoke came out of it. Madame Aurora waved her hands all around the crystal ball. Then everything stopped.

"Your locket is now cleansed," she said. "Cap'n Hornsby, please bring Mrs. McGraw her locket. Thank you, ladies and gentlemen, and good evening." She left the stage.

"A big hand for Madame Aurora," Cap'n Hornsby said, handing Mrs. McGraw the bag.

Mrs. McGraw reached inside and took out her locket. Then she shrieked.

"What is it, dear?" asked Mr. McGraw.

"My locket is empty!" Mrs. McGraw cried.

"Of course it's empty," replied her husband. "I just gave it to you last night. How could you have put a picture in it already?"

"I didn't put a picture in it, Charles," Mrs. McGraw explained. "I put the computer chip inside for safekeeping! I tried to tell you that before."

"Stop everything!" bellowed C. C. McGraw. "That fortune-teller is a thief! Hornsby, I want you to find that fortune-teller and my computer chip. If you don't, I'll be ruined! And I'll see to it personally that you and this boat never sail again!"

"That's our cue, gang," Fred said. "Mr. McGraw, don't worry about a thing. Mystery, Inc. is on the case!"

# Chapter 6

"There's no time to waste, so we'd better split up to look for clues," Fred said. "Daphne and I will see if we can find anything here in the theater."

"Scooby and I will check out the buffet," Shaggy suggested.

Fred, Daphne, and Velma gave him stern looks.

"Like, even fortune-tellers have to eat, right?" Shaggy said weakly.

"You two will come with me," Velma said. "We're going to the dressing room to see if we can find any sign of Madame Aurora."

"We'll meet back on deck as soon as we can," Fred said. "Now, let's get to work."

Fred and Daphne started looking around the stage. Velma, Shaggy, and Scooby walked behind the curtain and found a small dressing room backstage. On one side of the room was a table and a big mirror. Bright lightbulbs surrounded the mirror on three sides.

"This must be the makeup table," Velma noted. She looked in the mirror and saw a flowered curtain hanging in the reflection.

Velma walked over and whipped open the curtain.

"Ahhhhh!" screamed Shaggy and Scooby.

"What is it?" asked Velma.

"Nothing," Shaggy replied. "That was our just-in-case scream. You know, like just in case there was a monster in there or something."

Velma peeked into the small closet that was behind the curtain. It was empty. As Velma closed the curtain, she noticed a big section of it was missing.

"That's odd," she said. "Someone cut a piece of material out of this curtain. And why does it look so familiar to me?"

"Maybe the crystal ball has the answer," Shaggy suggested.

"Jinkies! That's it!" Velma exclaimed.

"What's it?" asked Shaggy.

"Now I know where I've seen this fabric before," Velma said. "Madame Aurora's scarf!"

"You mean she liked her scarf so much, she made Cap'n Hornsby get a curtain to match?" Shaggy wondered.

"I have a hunch she's not a real fortuneteller after all," Velma stated. "I'll bet she needed to make part of a costume in a hurry. Let's go find Fred and Daphne and let them know what we've found."

"We're right behind you, Velma," Shaggy said. They followed Velma out of the dressing room and back onto the stage.

The theater was empty now, but Madame Aurora's crystal ball was still onstage. Velma walked off the stage and up through the seats to the exit. Shaggy and Scooby stopped on the stage to look at the crystal ball.

"Hey, Scooby," Shaggy said. "Sit down and I'll tell you your fortune."

Shaggy gazed deeply into the crystal ball. "Like, I see wonderful things in your future," he said. "I see a long table with lots and lots of food on it. I see dishes piled high with pizza pies and chocolate-covered corn on the cob. I see . . . I see . . . I see someone standing behind you!

"Zoinks!" Shaggy exclaimed. "It's Madame Curtain-head!"

"Leave my crystal ball alone!" she ordered. "Or I will put a curse on you!"

"Like, let's get out of here, Scoob!" Shaggy yelled.

Madame Aurora chased them off the stage and through the narrow corridors on the

boat. Shaggy and Scooby found an open door. They ran into a small closet and closed the door behind them. Shaggy found the light switch and turned on the light.

"I think we lost her," Shaggy said. Then they heard a click and the sound of someone laughing. "Uh-oh, I think she found us," Shaggy said. He tried the door, but it was locked. “And now we’re locked inside this closet. Help!”

“Relp!” barked Scooby.

# Chapter 7

Shaggy and Scooby sat inside the locked closet.

"Man, why is it whenever we're trapped somewhere, I get incredibly hungry?" asked Shaggy. "I guess my stomach thinks I'll never eat again."

Scooby's ears suddenly perked up.

"You okay, pal?" asked Shaggy.

"Relp!" barked Scooby. "Rin rere!"

"Face it, Scoob," Shaggy said. "We're trapped in here forever. They'll never find us."

They heard another clicking sound, and

suddenly, the door opened. Daphne, Fred, Velma, and Cap'n Hornsby stood outside in the hallway.

"Shaggy! Scooby!" Daphne cried.

"Raphne!" Scooby said. He stood up and gave her a big Scooby hug and a kiss.

"We were looking all over for you two," Fred said.

"Well, we've been right here the whole time," Shaggy said. "How long has it been? A day? A week?"

"Try five minutes," Velma said.

"How did you end up in the crew's coat closet?" Cap'n Hornsby asked.

"Madame Aurora chased us and locked us inside," Shaggy explained.

"Well, why don't you two come out of there now?" asked Daphne.

"Just as soon as I finish finding the shortest way to the kitchen," Shaggy said.

"And how are you going to do that?" asked Velma.

"From this map on the back of the door," replied Shaggy.

"There's no map on the back of that door," said Cap'n Hornsby. He went inside and took a look. "That's funny," he said. "This map has a route to the theater and dressing room highlighted."

"That *is* funny," Shaggy said, chuckling. "Boy, that's a real knee-slapper." He and

Scooby laughed, then stopped abruptly. "I don't get it."

"Shaggy, Cap'n Hornsby meant that it's unusual for a map to be on this door," Daphne said. "After all, the crew shouldn't need a map to get around the ship."

"Especially one showing how to get to the dressing room," added Velma.

"This is an important clue, gang," Fred confirmed.

Suddenly, Scooby perked up his ears again.

"Ruh?" he said. He turned his head a little to listen to something.

"What is it, Scoob?" asked Shaggy.

"Rhhhh," Scooby said. "Risten."

The gang heard the faint sound of static coming from somewhere inside the room.

"I think that sound's coming from one of the coats," Daphne said. The gang started looking through the coats.

"I found it!" Velma said. She held up a small black box with a tiny earphone attached.

"What is it?" asked Shaggy.

"It's a radio transmitter," Velma said.

"Like, for listening to football games without being caught?" said Shaggy.

"Or listening and talking to someone else without being caught," Fred said.

"Now that we found this clue," Velma said, "I have a hunch that our phony fortune-teller is about to have a change of fortune herself."

"Velma's right," Fred declared. "It's time to set a trap."

# Chapter 8

"The only way we'll get Madame Aurora to come out of hiding is to make her think she has the wrong computer chip," Fred reasoned. "And that's where we need your help, Cap'n Hornsby."

"What can I do?" he asked.

"Announce that Madame Aurora has decided to do a special show in ten minutes," Fred said.

"And I'll take care of getting the McGraws there," Velma added. She left with Cap'n Hornsby.

"Now here's what we're going to do," Fred began.

"Hold on there, Fred-a-roony," Shaggy said. "If this plan includes me and Scooby getting close to that freaky fortune-teller, then you'd better count us out."

"But you haven't even heard it yet," Daphne said.

"It doesn't matter," Shaggy said. "There's no way we're getting involved in this one."

"How about you, Scooby?" Daphne asked. "Would you help out for, oh, say, a Scooby Snack?"

"Runh-unh," he declared.

"See? I told you," Shaggy said. "There's absolutely nothing you can say to make Scooby change his mind."

"How about two?" asked Daphne.

"Rokay!" barked Scooby. Daphne tossed the Scooby Snacks into the air. Scooby gobbled them down.

"Sold out for a Scooby Snack," Shaggy sighed.

"Here's the plan," Fred said. "Scooby, you're going to pretend to be Madame Aurora. Shaggy, you'll need to do Scooby's voice from behind the curtain. I'll hide back there with you. And when the real Madame Aurora shows up, we'll grab her."

"I'll take Scooby to the dressing room to get ready," Daphne said.

"Shaggy, you come with me," Fred said.

A few minutes later Velma led the McGraws into the theater along with Cap'n Hornsby. A few other passengers followed.

"I hope this little plan of yours works," Mr. McGraw said. "Though I don't see how a bunch of kids will be able to capture an industrial spy."

"Charles, you did say earlier that you had a good feeling about these young people," Mrs. McGraw reminded him. "Let's give them a chance."

"Very well," Mr. McGraw agreed. "Where do you want us?"

"Sit where you were sitting before," Velma said. "And wait for your cue." She sat down next to the McGraws. Cap'n Hornsby walked down to the stage.

"Ladies and gentlemen," he announced. "Please welcome back our favorite fortune-teller, Madame Aurora!"

Scooby-Doo walked out from behind the curtain. He wore the dressing room curtain over his head like a shawl. He wore a towel around his body like a smock. He bowed to the audience, and his shawl started to slip off. He raised his paw to grab the shawl, and the towel fell off his shoulder.

"Like, ladies and gentlemen," Shaggy said from behind the curtain. He disguised his voice and did his best to sound like a fortune-teller. "Is there someone out there who would like their fortune told?"

Mr. McGraw raised his hand slowly and stood up. Scooby-Doo pretended to see something in the crystal ball.

"Zoinks! I mean, oh my," Shaggy said as Scooby gazed deeper into the crystal ball. "You have lost something very valuable."

"Actually, Madame Aurora, I haven't," Mr. McGraw said. "The thing I thought I'd lost, I actually found. It's right here." He reached into his pocket and took out the ring box. "See?"

"Impossible!" screeched someone from the back of the theater. It was the real Madame Aurora! She ran down onto the stage and looked up at Mr. McGraw.

"You can't fool me, McGraw!" she hissed. "I have the computer chip and you know it!"

"I thought you did, Madame Aurora," Mr. McGraw replied. "But I was mistaken. I had given my wife the wrong chip for safekeeping."

"Now!" Fred whispered to Shaggy behind the curtain.

"Now!" Shaggy yelled in his fortune-teller voice.

Madame Aurora turned as Fred and Shaggy ran out from behind the curtain. Fred grabbed Scooby's cape and tried to throw it over Madame Aurora. She jumped out of the way and knocked Scooby into the table with the crystal ball. Scooby lost his balance and tumbled onto the crystal ball as it rolled. Soon he was rolling all over the stage on top of the ball.

"Relp! Raggy!" he yelled, rolling around crazily.

Shaggy and Fred dived out of the way as Scooby came toward them. Madame Aurora turned to run, but Scooby was coming too fast. He rolled right into the fortune-teller and knocked her down like a bowling pin.

"Way to go, Scooby-Doo!" Shaggy called. "You did it!"

"Now let's see who's really under this costume," Fred said.

# Chapter 9

Cap'n Hornsby and the McGraws all gathered around Madame Aurora.

"Why don't you do the honors, Mr. McGraw?" asked Fred.

"It would be my pleasure," Mr. McGraw replied. He reached down and grabbed Madame Aurora's scarf. When he lifted it off, the fortune-teller's mask came off, too.

"Floyd Mathewson!" exclaimed Cap'n Hornsby.

"Just as we suspected," Velma said.

"You did?" asked Mrs. McGraw. "How did you know?"

"It wasn't easy," Daphne began. "We knew that there were a lot of people on this boat who had a score to settle with your husband."

"And when we found the flowered dressing room curtain, we knew that our fortune-teller was a phony," Velma said.

"At first we thought it was Dorothy Cobb," Fred said. "She seemed pretty serious about wanting to stop Mr. McGraw."

"But she was on deck being seasick during the show," Daphne pointed out. "We saw her just as we were going downstairs, remember?"

"That's right!" Mr. McGraw remembered.

"So that left Floyd Mathewson and Mr. Wagner," Velma continued. "The next clue we found was the map to the theater on the closet door."

"We figured that someone who worked

on the boat wouldn't need a map," Fred said. "He should know his way around. Which suggested that Floyd Mathewson was behind all of this."

"But then we realized that someone who knew the boat had to draw the map for Floyd Mathewson," Daphne said. "And that this same someone was able to get secret information about the passengers. He was also in a position to call the *real* Madame Aurora and tell her the show was canceled. Then the fake Madame Aurora — Floyd Mathewson — could take her place."

"Of course, Mr. Wagner!" exclaimed Cap'n Hornsby. "But how did they find out so much about the passengers?"

"Mr. Wagner overheard your conversations with passengers as they boarded," Fred explained. "He used his mini security radio to transmit the information to Floyd Mathewson. Floyd then used the information in his fortune-teller act."

"That must be how he knew where the chip was!" Mrs. McGraw said. "He must have overheard me tell the captain where I put the computer chip."

"And he picked Mr. McGraw's pocket

early in the evening so he could get his wallet," Velma added.

"Once he had your locket," Daphne continued, "Floyd used the glowing crystal ball and smoke to distract us. He opened the bag and took out the computer chip."

"You'd better track down that no-good Wagner, Captain," Mrs. McGraw said.

"We're on a boat, Mrs. McGraw," Cap'n Hornsby replied. "He's not going anywhere."

"And neither are you, Mr. Mathewson, until you return my computer chip," Mr. McGraw said.

Floyd Mathewson reached into his pocket. He took out the computer chip and gave it to Mr. McGraw.

"But if that's not the real chip," Floyd Mathewson said, "what's the big deal?"

"I'm afraid I misled you a bit," Mr. McGraw answered. "It is the real chip. And the only one of its kind."

Mr. McGraw turned and looked at the gang. "Kids," he said, "I owe you and your dog a big thank-you. And for starters, I want you to know that I'm going to put this computer chip into the world's newest, fastest, and smartest computer: the Scooby 1000."

"You forgot one important feature," Shaggy suggested.

"What's that?" asked Mr. McGraw.

"Like, it'll also be the hungriest!" joked Shaggy.

Everyone laughed and looked at Scooby-Doo.

"Scooby-Dooby-Doo!" he barked.

# About the Author

As a boy, James Gelsey used to run home from school to watch the Scooby-Doo cartoons on television (only after finishing his homework). Today, he still enjoys watching them with his wife and two daughters. He also has a real dog named Scooby who loves nothing more than a good Scooby Snack!